# I Should Have Told

—————————————— by Omaira

DORRANCE
PUBLISHING CO
EST. 1920
PITTSBURGH, PENNSYLVANIA 15238

Dorrance Publishing Co
585 Alpha Drive
Suite 103
Pittsburgh, PA 15238
Visit our website at *www.dorrancebookstore.com*

ISBN: 978-1-6386-7059-9
eISBN: 978-1-6386-7881-6

# Dedication

To my Granny, my Mima: my first true love, my heart, and my soul. You will forever be missed. Te Quiero Mucho, Pero de Verdad (I Love You Much, But for Real).

To my Hubby: my number-one supporter, the one who always believes in me no matter what I do. Thank you for putting up with my craziness and silliness. I can always be the real me with you. There has never been you and me; it's always been US. My backbone, my voice of reason, my forever love, and my always protector.

To my cousin-daughter: Ever since you were born, you were mine. Through the good and bad times in our lives, you were mine. Till we stop breathing, you are mine.

To the few I shared my first pages with, my pictures and even some ideas, sorry to have kept you in the dark and waiting. I value your input. Even if you didn't know exactly what I was doing, I'm pretty sure you had a slight inkling. You know me well. Thanks for dealing with my erratic mood swings, my manic ups and especially my depressive lows. As I always say, I am probably tri-polar (if that's a true diagnosis); someday I promise to get treatment. Until then, you're stuck with me.

To the friends and family that knew some things but didn't know all, it was my choice not to tell and for that I apologize. To those that I did tell and nothing was done, I forgive you.

And especially to all the girls that never told, to the ones that did. To the girls that were believed, to the ones that weren't, know that you did nothing wrong. Learn to forgive yourselves and most importantly the ones that hurt you.

# Contents

*The imagination of a child is a vast open field of love, peace and perfection.*

*Anything possible, everything beautiful and clean.*
*So powerful our minds, with unique arrays of shapes*
*and forms in colors that have not been designed.*
*Each child's mind is full of uniqueness, visions of what the future will be like.*
*To take that away from a child is the ultimate betrayal,*
*turning beauty into pain and bitterness.*
*Eventually love turns into anger, peace into contemplation.*
*Innocence turns into revenge.*
*Revenge turns splashes of beautiful blues, yellows, pinks and greens into*
*dark blots of blacks, grays and reds.*
*Ah, but the bold powerful shades of red!*
*Red is strong, undefeatable, resilient.*
*Strength and resilience will determine how it will all end.*

# Book One:
## —— The Beginning

A story about lost innocence and the will to fight

Based on true events

# Chapter One
## —————— Puerto Rico

Why am I here again? Never the deviation. Mrs. Carmen is in the kitchen cooking her signature white rice and beans. Every day the same routine, every day the same sides with different meats. One day pork chops, one day chicken, another steak. But always with white rice and always with beans. Doesn't she get tired of the same routine? I know I do.

The kitchen is small but tidy. A stove, fridge and sink with a few cabinets along one wall. There's a square metal table with silver legs and four matching chairs on another wall, a gray metal door with a peeling gate that remains open all day leading out to the porch. The decor is overwhelming splashes of flowers. A four-piece canister set, rug in front of the sink, the window curtains and table placemats, all flowers.

Mrs. Carmen is short and round and, in my eyes, old. She has gray hair styled in a bun. She wears no makeup, no perfume. I know she doesn't wear perfume because she smells like rubbing alcohol and menthol cream. The smell is so powerful it stings my eyes if I'm too close. She must own a closet full of colorful housecoats. The ones with flowers that have snaps down the front and pockets on the sides. I wonder every day how many does she have. I tried counting them but they all look alike so I lost count a long time ago. She wears slippers all day, never shoes. Why doesn't she wear anything else? Maybe that's what old people wear to cook and clean all day.

# Omaira

She barely speaks to me but she talks to herself. I just sit and wait. I wait all day with this talking, cooking, cleaning old lady. Mrs. Carmen is my babysitter. She watches me while my grandmother works. I sit at the kitchen table for hours every day just looking at her moving around the small kitchen, listening to her but not knowing what she mumbles about. I have nothing else to do.

She has a husband. He is usually gone when I am dropped off in the morning but sometimes he comes home before I am picked up. He comes in through the kitchen door, sits and stares. Mrs. Carmen immediately puts his food on the table. I wonder if she is a mind reader. How does she know he is hungry as soon as he walks in the house?

He's old too and doesn't smell any better than his wife. He is tall and thin with a slight stoop to his back. He's all gray with bushy eyebrows. He wears jeans and button-down shirts. His skin is dark and weathered, wrinkled like worn leather. Maybe he works out in the sun and sweats all day or maybe he doesn't wear cologne either. He doesn't talk to himself like his wife does; actually he doesn't talk at all. He just stares with dark eyes that barely blink. I feel like he is trying to read my mind or look into my soul. I don't know his name or anything about him. He stares and I stare back wondering what he is thinking about. I say hi but he doesn't respond. Eventually I look away. I think he is creepy. He reminds me of a zombie, a dead zombie that does not speak or blink but eats. That makes me giggle. My imagination runs away from me sometimes.

One day, as I'm sitting in my usual kitchen chair watching Mrs. Carmen cook, he comes in. She goes to serve his food and he tells her he is not hungry. I stare up at him thinking this is the first time I hear his voice. He has a low, raspy monotone voice that does not display emotion. He tone is gruff with no kindness to it. He looks down at me with his dark eyes piercing and asks if I want to go see his crabs. I am unsure of the invitation and look at Mrs. Carmen for permission. I question her silently. She looks away without acknowledging if I can or cannot go so I don't move from my seat. I look back and forth from her to him, at his waiting dark eyes and at her back, not understanding why she is ignoring me.

Seconds pass by feeling like minutes and I don't know what to do. I stay seated. He starts walking towards the back of the house, his eyes instructing me to follow him. I've never seen live crabs before and I really wanted to see them. Mrs. Carmen is not saying not to go, she is not saying or doing anything so I stand up still looking at her for confirmation. She does not acknowledge me and he is getting closer to the door, seemingly not caring if I follow or not. My curiosity won and I quickly catch up to him to go outside. Not knowing that following him would change my life forever.

I have been told that my curiosity and imagination would either get me in trouble or make me famous. I prefer the latter, of course. I am a friendly, happy, funny but curious and mischievous little girl. I am outspoken and want to know the answer to everything. Some will even say I was nosy, always trying to listen to other people's conversations, often adding my opinion. Although friendly, I was also the loner. I needed no other kids to play with; I had all my imaginary friends and myself. I have dark mysterious eyes. Eyes that do not lie, you can tell my moods when looking at them. I have a cute round face, a button nose and a cheeky smile with dimples. A contagious laugh that doesn't stop once it starts. I love wearing my long unruly curly hair loose down my back, always wanting to run around, didn't mind playing in the dirt, and getting dirty. I am not the type of girl to have tea parties and play with dolls. These are characteristics that I will never outgrow. Generally I am a bright, happy, healthy child, not skinny but not fat, I would say chunky and squeezable.

My mother was a child when she had me and my grandmother helped out as much as she could. My mother was fifteen and my father was seventeen. My grandmother forced my father to marry my mother, although he had another girl pregnant at the same time. A true gunshot wedding. That marriage only lasted a few months so I was practically raised by my grandmother.

My mother and I lived with her until my mother decided to move to New York. I was devastated that I was leaving but I was promised to spend every summer with my grandmother.

And every summer I flew back to Puerto Rico to spend it with my favorite person in the world. I traveled alone on American Airlines on a huge plane.

The stewardess sat me in the front row near her. She got me snacks and pinned little gray wings on my shirt. I loved to fly alone. I watched movies and I behaved because I was a big girl. When we landed, the stewardess took me directly to the arms of my waiting grandmother, whom I called Mima. She told me that I started calling her that because I could not pronounce her real name, so Mima it was. She was the love of my life. She had always given me all the attention I wanted and everything I needed. I was the happiest little girl when I was with her. I had no worries. No one could hurt me when I was with her. She was my protector, my heart, my everything! I could tell her whatever was bothering me and she would fix it. She was the strongest person I knew. She was larger than life, a fighter, and I knew she would always keep me safe. So why didn't I ever say anything to her? I question this every day of my life.

I will always remember that dreadful day but it didn't start off as dreadful. It was a beautiful, sunny, warm summer day. The sun was shining; the sky was blue with fat, fluffy clouds that I tried to touch. Mima had a candy apple-red hatchback. She liked fast cars and loved to drive even faster. Going around the turns without breaking. Laughing loud and singing to whatever music was playing on the radio. I would never sit in the seats, not in the front or back. My spot was lying in the hatchback area, looking out the glass up at the sky. Trying to sing along, laughing when we went fast and trying to grab the clouds. Mima's laugh was hearty and deep. We laughed at nothing in particular, just enjoyed our time together. For as long as I remember, I was always a dreamer. I enjoyed the peace and quiet, the wonder of all things; I imagined myself being a superhero, a defender of mankind, a happy, content fantasist.

Just like many other mornings, Mima dropped me off at Mrs. Carmen's house. I waved until I couldn't see the bright red car any longer. I knew it would be seven hours before she would come back for me. Seven hours when all I did was daydream, wonder and wait. That day was just like any other, except that Mrs. Carmen's husband came home early, wasn't hungry and actually spoke to me.

As I followed him out the back door, I was amazed at the vastness of the back of the house. I had never been back there. There seemed to be miles and miles of trees. All kinds of trees! There were banana trees, mango trees, and

Spanish lime bushes that we called quenepas. There were hundreds if not thousands of plants as far as I could see. I was amazed at all the vegetation and fruits but I didn't touch anything without being told. I obediently followed him through the trees, trying to keep up so I would not get lost. Focusing on my steps as his seemed to be getting faster. Did he not know I had shorter legs? I had to keep up or surely I would disappear, never to be found. We walked for a long time. I lost any sense of time. We could have been walking minutes or hours.

Finally he stopped and turned to me. There on the ground was a hole, a small cave-like structure that I had never seen. Picking up a branch from the ground, he stuck it in the small cave and wiggled it around. After a few minutes, he pulled it out and a huge blue crab was holding on to the branch. I screamed with glee. The crab looked mean with beady eyes coming out of its head and a small moving mouth. Did crabs have teeth? I wasn't sure but it did have huge snapping claws that would surely rip my fingers off if I touched it. The crab seemed to be clawing directly at me. I was scared that it would pinch me and I jumped back.

Jumping back, I bumped into him. I did not realize he was so close to me. The crab fell to the ground, quickly scurrying sideways. Now I screamed thinking it was coming my way, but he picked me up and held me tight. For the second time, I heard his voice: "This will be our secret. Don't tell anyone that I brought you back here because you will get in trouble. You are too young to be looking for crabs. I will bring you back to see them, maybe even take some to cook, but only if you are a good girl and never tell anyone. I will bring you back." And with those last words, he carried me back to the house.

Days passed and I didn't see him again. I fell into the same daily routine. I thought about going into the trees again. I imagined it a vast jungle where I would get lost and had to fend for myself. I saw myself fighting off wild animals and surviving by eating the fruits. I imagined me catching the crabs all by myself. Fighting them with sticks and making sure I saved them for dinner. Did I want to go see them again? Of course I did! They were dangerous and untamable and delicious. I really wanted to go back. Then one day I did.

We started walking through the trees again, me concentrating on his footsteps. This time we took another path. I'm not sure but I think we went further and it took longer until we found another little cave. It was not the same one so I imagined the entire land being full of caves. This time he gave me my own branch. As I bent down, I felt his hands on my waist. Surely he was holding me so I would not fall or to pick me up if I got attacked. His hands begin to tighten and move up and down, in circles, slowly reaching my chest. It felt funny but I tried to ignore it and concentrate on my task. I heard his breathing getting louder and felt it hot on my neck.

For some reason I didn't move, I didn't breathe and I stopped thinking about the crab that I so much anticipated catching. What was happening? Nobody ever touched me like that and why was he breathing so hard? "I'm ready to go back to the house," I said.

Without a word, he picked me up and carried me out of the trees. Once we reached the back of the house, he took me to the outdoor latrine. The structure was made of cement with a tin roof. There was a toilet, a concrete shower and a sink. "Let me wash your hands and face, you got dirty," he whispered. He wipes my hands with his and then my eyes, my cheeks and finally my mouth. This was strange because I didn't remember touching anything to dirty my face. His fingers caressed my lips until they were inside of my mouth. I just stood there not knowing why his fingers were in and out of my mouth. Maybe I did get dirt on my face and in my mouth.

I looked up at him and saw that his eyes were closed, his face serious, concentrating. Suddenly, his eyes opened and bore into mine. "Go back in the house, now!" I jumped and tears began to burn my eyes. "Don't you start crying and don't tell anyone where you were. You will get in a lot of trouble and won't be able to come here anymore!" With that I ran back into the house and sat at the kitchen table with my head down on my arms. Confused and scared that I was going to get in trouble. That somehow Mrs. Carmen was going to tell my grandmother that I had misbehaved, although I did not think I did anything bad. I wasn't sure what I did wrong but I knew something was wrong, so I said nothing. The last thing I wanted was my grandmother to be upset with me so I remained quiet on the ride home. She questioned why I was not talking, as this was not my normal behavior. I lied and told her I didn't feel good. And that's when I began keeping secrets.

# Chapter Two
## ——— My Secrets to Keep

My rides to Mrs. Carmen's became quiet. One day I arrived at the house and I noticed how small it really was. It was a plain concrete square, painted in Caribbean mint green. It had a small porch in the front of the house built from ugly old cinderblocks. It had a white chipped iron gate, two rusty white metal rockers and a small side table, with lots of flowerpots full of sad, half-dead flowers and plants. I realized the inside was just as sad, albeit spotless. The small flowery kitchen, a living room that no one used with flower-pattern sofas covered in clear plastic. There was a large scratched shelf full of little vases with plastic flowers, ceramic dogs and angels, a large console television with more junk on top of it, everything containing different-size lace dollies. There were two bedrooms; one belonged to Mrs. Carmen and her husband and the other belonged to her son. I had never met their son, I guess he was grown and did not live there anymore. Those doors were always closed and I was not allowed in those rooms.

Then there was the outside latrine, all made of dark gray concrete. I was glad that I didn't have to use that latrine at night. I would have rather peed my pants than to go out there in the dark. Today nothing held the same wonder and excitement as before. Now it was dark with scary twists of trees, no grass, just dirt grounds full of strange smells. Smells that reminded me of rotten leaves, and, the green and black mildew that grew up the walls when things were wet. Brown mud in puddles that never dried, the sun never penetrating. Now I noticed the creepy places where things could hide, creepy things like him.

Several weeks passed by and I didn't see him. He didn't come home early to eat. Once I was picked up, I would run to the car. I started talking and laughing again. I enjoyed my time with my Mima again. I didn't say I felt sick anymore. I just wanted to ride in the back of the hatchback and look up at the sky. Everything was normal again until one day it wasn't.

I was dropped off one morning and he was there. I immediately froze when I saw him sitting across from my normal chair in the kitchen table. It seemed as if Mrs. Carmen was always in front of the stove. Didn't she do anything else? He told me to go with him to the living room to watch television. I slowly rose and went. I sat as close to the sofa arm as I could so he could have space to sit on the other side or even on the other sofa, but he sat near me. He was so close that I could not move an inch; even if I stood up we would touch. I could smell him. He smelled like the outdoors, like the trees and dirt. I could smell his breath, coffee mixed with the oatmeal he ate for breakfast. I felt my stomach tighten and churn like I wanted to throw up. I started sweating, feeling the heat radiating off his body. I didn't know what that feeling was at the time. Later I realized it was disgust mixed with fear.

I stayed as still as one of the ceramic figurines on top of the television. His hands grazed my neck, back, slowly moving down to my thigh. As his hand reached and rested on my inner thigh, I couldn't hold my bladder anymore. Hot urine began to run down my legs, spreading to the seat of my pants and finally making a puddle on the plastic covering the sofa. I didn't move, couldn't move. I didn't feel or hear him getting up and getting Mrs. Carmen to clean me up. I didn't feel Mrs. Carmen pushing me into a corner so she could clean my mess, leaving me standing in my wet clothes. And I definitely didn't realize that wetting myself was a horrible mistake.

Mrs. Carmen rushed in with a bucket of water and a rag to wipe her sofas. I stood for what seemed like an eternity, watching her wipe the plastic and the urine that dripped to the floor. She dipped the rag into the soapy water over and over until everything was cleaned. I was so cold that I began to shake, shivering uncontrollably although it was a hot, humid day. My pants were soaked all the way down to my socks. I was so ashamed and scared. I never soiled myself. I never had accidents.

She looked at me and I knew she was angry. Her eyes demanding an explanation and her mouth set into a thin hard line. I prayed she called my grandmother so she could pick me up. She would pick me up and I would tell her everything so I would never have to return to this stupid house. I could go to work with her. I pictured us together at the restaurant where she was a waitress. I could help bring the food to her customers. Her customers were kind and treated me so nice when I visited. The owner always brought me cake and soda pop. I could sit at the counter all day just like I sat here in the kitchen. I promised myself that I would be no bother, no bother at all.

Mrs. Carmen took me to the latrine to wash me up. She took all my clothes off and made me shower in the concrete stall. All my clothes were wet—my pants, panties, socks and even my shirt. I took the washrag full of soap and ran it through my body fast and hard. I tried to wash away my shame with the cold water. I was too ashamed to even cry, although that was what I felt like doing. I wanted to cry and scream for my grandmother to come pick me up. I wanted to run outside and wait for her in the street. But I was naked and cold.

Mrs. Carmen wrapped me up in a towel and scooted me into her bedroom. "Stay here until I wash your clothes and hang them up to dry. You are lucky it's hot, if not you would be wearing wet clothes! And you are never allowed on my sofas again, you are a bad girl!" she screamed at me. I sat there on the edge of the bed wrapped in the scratchy towel, trembling from the inside out. I shook so hard I felt the bed move and the room spin. Eventually I fell asleep, cold and alone in the strange room.

I was dreaming ants were crawling over me. Hot red fiery ants, biting and stinging, millions of them all over my feet and legs, crawling higher and higher until they were all over my body. They were running up my stomach, my arms, face and hair. I felt them biting me. I swatted them, trying to get them off of me, but more would come. I could feel them running on my face, trying to get in my mouth; I stopped breathing. I wanted to scream but didn't dare open my mouth. But they still got in, I felt them going down my throat. Suddenly there were so many of them I could not close my mouth; I began to gag, my jaw started to hurt. I tried to scream but no sound came out. I felt the tears running down my face, my hair getting caught on something as I fought to get them off of me. I grabbed my hair to set myself free but they were everywhere. My scalp was on fire and I couldn't break free. Were there so many ants that they could drag me away? Where did they come from? Why were they on me?

Finally I was able to open my eyes and tried to focus through my burning tears. He was standing in front of me. He was the cause of this pain and I didn't understand. I realized there were no ants. He had his hands wrapped in my hair. His fists were balled up, pulling and pulling, harder and harder. I tried to scream but only a muffled sound came out. My jaw felt as if it was being pulled apart and I didn't know why. I felt something sliding in and out of my mouth, reaching the back of my throat and I couldn't stop it, I couldn't scream or breathe. I held on to my hair with both hands, trying to pry his hands. With tears running down my face I closed my eyes, wishing it would stop. I thought he was going to rip the hair off my scalp. Mentally I screamed, *Get off my hair, let go of my mouth, I can't breathe, I'm going to die!* I was starting to see black spots swirling in front of me. I felt like I was falling, everything fading. Then it stopped as fast as it started.

Everything was hurting, every part of my body, especially my head and my jaw. What did he do to me? What did he put in my mouth? Was he trying to kill me? What did I do? Oh my God, then I remembered, I peed on the sofa and on the floor, I peed my clothes. This was the punishment for wetting myself. I told myself I was such a bad girl and I promised never to do it again.

I vaguely remember dosing off until Mrs. Carmen came back with my clothes. They were not fully dried but I was relieved to put them back on. I didn't know what I was feeling. I didn't hear anything that was said to me. I slowly dressed and walked outside. I sat alone on the porch waiting to be picked up. Looking at nothing with tears running down my face in my damp clothes. I wasn't hot nor I was cold. I felt nothing but the pain in my head and face. I tried to bury the memory and pain deep inside. I kept telling myself it was a bad dream, nothing happened. Glimpses would pop up and I would try to push them back down. I don't know why the punishment was so harsh. I didn't mean to pee myself but I promised not to do it again. I promised not to be bad again. I would listen and be a good girl for now on. I would do what I had to do so I wouldn't be punished like that again.

When my grandmother picked me up, I could see the worry on her face and then anger. "What happened to her, why is she wet and crying!" she demanded. I sensed Mrs. Carmen was angry as well but she would not dare raise her voice at my grandmother. Few ever did. She told her that I had intentionally wet my clothes because I was too lazy to go to the bathroom since she let me watch television. Thankfully she had plastic on her sofas; if not they would be ruined, she insisted. She said if this happened again she could not watch me again. She was not going to watch a baby. I could see the doubt and concern in my grandmother's face as she stood there with one hand on her waist, one leg forward like a tigress ready to pounce. My grandmother's stance scared and made me feel safe at the same time. "Are you okay?" she asked me. I looked at the ground and shook my head. "I want to go home. I'm cold and my head hurts," I replied quietly. I knew that if I told her what happened she would drag Mrs. Carmen and her husband down the road. She would surely punch and kick them and hurt them. Hurt them like he hurt me. She would cut them with her scissors that she always carried in her purse. Beat them with the bat she had in the back of the car. Pound them until they were nothing but bloody mounds. That's what she would do to anyone that hurt me. And yet I remained quiet. I felt ashamed and dirty.

I cried myself to sleep that night. Woke up with my eyes and face swollen, my head still hurt and I told my grandmother that I didn't want to go to Mrs. Carmen's house. She asked me over and over why I wet myself, was everything okay, not to lie to her. And over and over I told her it was an accident and I would never do it again. I told her I was fine. She wasn't mad at me for wetting myself but I could tell that she was worried. I could also tell that she didn't believe me, she knew I was keeping something from her, but how could she ever suspect it was the worst thing that could happen to a young girl? To my chagrin, I had to go back.

"I have to work a few hours but I will be back early. You call the restaurant if anything happens. Do you understand?" my grandmother told Mrs. Carmen with the sternest attitude I had ever seen. Mrs. Carmen just nodded and took me inside. I looked back and my grandmother was still standing there, this time with both her fists on her hips and her head cocked to the side. She looked like a mad bull ready to charge, her eyebrows knitted together in thought, her eyes like slits and her lips pursed. I tried to smile at her but it didn't reach my face. I told myself that she knew. She read my mind and she knew.

"Sit down and don't start any trouble. I don't know what you told your grandmother but you better not tell any lies! I know how you little girls can be. And I don't want any trouble-making liars in my house," Mrs. Carmen hissed at me. I wanted to scream that her husband was a mean old smelly man. He was the troublemaker, not me. He pulled my hair and hurt me. He was the bad one, not me. I wanted to scream that I hated them and I didn't want to be there anymore. I wanted to tell my grandmother everything so she could get me out of here. But I didn't.

My grandmother picked me up at lunchtime that day. She told Mrs. Carmen that I would only be there until the following Friday. She would no longer be taking care of me. Mrs. Carmen looked perturbed and I looked smug. I knew my grandmother wouldn't let anyone hurt me. I knew she would protect me.

In the car I asked my grandmother if it was true that I didn't have to come back. "No, you don't have to come back. I'm not going to work anymore and you can stay home with me," she said. I was so happy! I smiled and talked and laughed all the way home. I rode in the hatch of the car and talked to the clouds as if I had not seen them in years. "Mima, how many days until next Friday?" I asked her. "Two days this week and then five next week and that's it," she responded. Some of my worry returned, that was a long time to me. Two days then five seemed like a lifetime. I closed my eyes and prayed that he would not be there those days. Before bed, I prayed to Baby Jesus that those days would go fast and that I would not have to see him. I prayed for next Friday.

I woke up with a tummy ache. It was a different type of pain. It felt hot like I ate coals and swallowed them whole. My chest felt like it was full of drummers, beating hard and furious. Sweat beaded my forehead and dripped down my back. My breathing came fast and hard. I knew I didn't want to go to the sitter's. I couldn't move, I felt paralyzed, my legs and arms not responding to my brain. I couldn't lift my body out of the bed. My warm pink comforter was holding me captive. I felt it gripping me and getting tighter, warning me that if I tried to move it would strangle me. I closed my eyes tight and laid very still. I refused to move.

I usually woke up early to dress and go into the kitchen before Mima did. I tried to beat her so I could run outside to the porch and scream at the school kitchen lady across the street. The elementary school was directly across from our house. I had never been inside the school because I was too young. It was a one-floor building with lots of little windows and a tin roof. The flat structure that looked more like one big rectangle than it did a school. It took up half of the block and painted a light blue color.

The kitchen door was always open and I could see Rosita cooking for the kids. Rosita was young, maybe in her twenties. She was tall and thin with dark brown hair always up in a ponytail. She had matching big round brown eyes and a silly twisted smile like she knew some good jokes. As soon as I saw her I screamed out to her, "Rosita, I want some cheese and crackers!" She turned her back to me but I knew she was laughing and pretending to ignore me so I could keep calling her. I screamed louder and told her that I knew she could hear me! She turned laughing, as I knew she would. With a huge smile she ran across the street with some saltines and cubes of cheddar cheese wrapped in a paper towel. I never wanted the breakfast she was cooking, crackers and cheese were my favorite. With a big wave, she ran back to her kitchen while I sat on the porch nibbling on my snack like a little mouse until Mima was ready.

I lay in my normal spot in the back of the car on our way to the sitter's. I kept asking Mima why did she have to work for so long. I told her I didn't like it at Mrs. Carmen's house anymore but I didn't tell her why. She told me to call her at the restaurant if I didn't feel good and I agreed. I knew I wouldn't call her, why bother her? I remained quiet for the duration of the ride and just looked up at the sky, daydreaming about my new baby chicks that hatched the night before. Little fluffy yellow puffballs and I couldn't wait to play with them. Mima said I had to be very gentle with them. I fed the grown chickens every day. I threw cornmeal at them and watched them run around squawking. They didn't like me much because sometimes I chased them with a stick. I was not supposed to but it was fun to see them running all over the place and hearing them squeal. I never hit them, though; I would definitely get in trouble for that. I laugh quietly at the memory.

# Chapter Three

―――――――――― Countdown

Seven days. That was how many days I counted before I could be home with Mima and not come here anymore. Today Mrs. Carmen was not really speaking to me. She was cleaning like a maniac, more than usual. Scrubbing every surface in the kitchen with the same rag, going in circles, so hard that her knuckles were white. She scrubbed the stove, the cabinets and counters; she wiped the table around me, 'round and 'round, and then started on the cabinets again. I knew she was angry but at what, I didn't know. Maybe she was still mad at me for peeing on her sofas. I didn't even care anymore. I began to get angry too. I felt like she was ignoring me, why was I even here? I just wanted to go home.

This place was stupid and dumb and she was not taking care of me, so I pushed my coloring book and crayons on the floor. They scattered and rolled everywhere. Mrs. Carmen jumped so high; I thought she was going to touch the ceiling. I didn't move to pick anything up. I sat there with a smirk on my face, daring her to call my grandmother. There was anger radiating from my being, something I never felt before. I felt a darkness and meanness that I had never experienced. I wanted her to get mad, I wanted to taunt her and I wanted to make her cry. Maybe it was the look in my eyes that made her step back. I imagined my eyes turning red with flames shooting out at her. I saw Mrs.

Carmen burning. I saw her clothes catching fire, incinerating the material, orange flames licking at her skin, blistering and withering her flesh until her bones began to blacken. Whatever she saw in me, I could tell it scared her. She didn't ask me to pick up my mess; she quickly looked away and walked out of the kitchen, leaving me alone.

I was still smirking when I heard them arguing. I was glad they were fighting. I didn't care about them anymore. My face dropped when he came in the room and pulled me by my arm so hard I thought it was going to come off. He pulled me into a lopsided standing position and pushed me down to the floor. I fell on my knees. The only thing keeping me from smashing my face on the floor was my hand. "Pick your shit up, girl," he hissed. I felt my anger seething, getting darker inside. "You're hurting me, let me go!" I screamed. Instead of loosening his grip, he squeezed harder and I yelped. "I said pick your shit up, girl, and don't you dare scream at me because I will call your grandmother and tell her what you did to me. You are a bad girl and I will tell her. Who do you think she will believe? You??? I don't think so. No one believes bad lying little girls like you. No one!" At that moment, I knew he won. I felt all my anger turn into shame. My heat went out as if a cold bucket of water was poured on me. He was right. My grandmother would be ashamed of me. He would tell everyone and everyone would know what I did. No one would want to be near me, no one would love me. I quietly began to pick up my crayons, tears running down my face. I did bad things and I was a horrible girl.

Once I picked everything up, he sat on the chair and pulled me onto his lap. "Stop crying, little girl. You have to learn how to listen. You have to behave," he softly crooned. "I'm sorry I hollered at you but you have to be a good girl for me. Come here; let me make you feel better. Stop crying, little girl." He began rubbing my back, my shoulders, and my neck. I felt his sweaty hands roll over my arms. His fingers moved to my chest. He was holding me up with one hand on my back while the other was roaming all over my small body. He reached the bottom of my shirt and slightly lifted it just enough to creep his hand up my belly. His hands rubbed from side to side higher and higher until they reached my chest.

# I Should Have Told

I was never told that no one should ever touch my chest but I knew he was not supposed to be rubbing me. He jumped from one of my nonexistent breasts to the other, moving his fingers in circles. I was frozen with fear; I stopped crying but didn't move. He pinched my small nipples between two of his fingers and I whimpered. He slowly began rubbing lower until he reached the top of my pants. With one finger he began to test the tightness of the hem. He could not reach his hand inside my pants without taking them off. He continued to explore my upper thighs, my legs, my inner thighs and finally my private parts. I definitely knew that he should not be touching me there. Those were my private parts and they were mine only. I gasped and pushed his hands away. He roughly smacked my hands and grabbed me again.

This time he grabbed at me rougher and I felt something poking me on my bottom as I sat on his lap. He gripped me higher and closer to him, held me tighter while still rubbing my private area roughly. It began to hurt; I felt my jeans rubbing me, making my skin tender. I couldn't take it any longer. I dug my nails into his hands and with all my might jumped off his lap. I ran to a corner and stood there breathing hard and just stared at him like a feral cat ready to pounce if he got near me again. Thankfully he got up and walked away, leaving the room. I stood in the corner for a long time, not feeling safe to move. It was even longer before Mrs. Carmen came back in the kitchen. I can't remember how long I was standing in that corner, but I couldn't move. All I felt was an overwhelming hate coming from my heart. I was taught that hate was a bad thing. But I already did bad things so why not add hate to my list?

When my grandmother picked me up, I was still angry. I got in the car and barely spoke. That evening I went to play with my baby chicks. They were a soft yellow that reminded me of the morning sun. They were so soft and fluffy that I wondered if they had fur instead of feathers. There were seven chicks in total, all little fat, chirping round puffs. Watching them run around pecking at their powdery corn feed, tripping over each other made me laugh and I temporarily forgot about the bad. Mima showed me how to hold them. I held them softly in one hand and pet their fluffy head with my other. I had to be extra gentle because they were very fragile. I put my hand in the cage slowly to grab another chick and it pecked me so fast that I screamed and pulled my hand out. I slammed the cage shut to examine my hand. I had a pinprick of blood, that bastard really pecked me. I fed it and I was nice to it and it hurt me!

I opened the cage and grabbed the first chick I could and squeezed. The more it wiggled and tried to peck me, the harder I squeezed. I squeezed until it stopped chirping and it didn't move any longer. When I finally looked at my hand I realized that I had several red marks. As I was squeezing the chick, the others were busy pecking at my hand. Funny thing was that I didn't feel it, my hand was red and puffy but I felt nothing. I went in the house and got my grandmother's coffee thermos. Calmly I filled it with the chicks, one of top of the other. They chirped and squirmed but could not climb out. Lastly I dropped in the dead chick. All seven of them were in the thermos now. I screwed on the top, threw the thermos in the trash and went in the house.

Six days. I was counting down. Today I left my coloring book and crayons at home. I didn't bring anything to entertain myself. I wanted to be aware of where the grownups were in the house. On the ride over, it began to rain. The raindrops pinged loudly on the car windows and dripped down like fat teardrops. The clouds were dark, racing across the sky in wide circles. All of a sudden there was a bright flash of lightning across the sky that lit up all the trees. A loud clap of thunder came next. I felt the vibrations in my bones and the cold made my teeth chatter. Now I was not scared of lightning or thunder like most kids, I loved sitting outside watching the rain and especially storms. For some reason they relaxed me instead of making me nervous. My grandmother hated storms. She would turn off every television and cover all mirrors with sheets and towels. I never understood this but she would say that the television and mirrors were magnets for the lightning. Apparently electricity could travel through the television, although I had never seen this happen. Secretly I would hold a small mirror next to the window to see what would happen but nothing ever did. So I guess that's where I got my love of storms. Sitting in the dark, quietly looking out the window waiting for the storm to pass with everything turned off but my imagination.

# I Should Have Told

I ran from the car to the porch and still got drenched. I turned and waved back to my grandmother, who stayed in the car so she would not wet her work clothes. Mrs. Carmen ushered me inside. Today she was cooking a full breakfast of eggs, bacon, and potatoes. There was even a plate of fruit on the table and four glasses of fresh-squeezed orange juice. I wondered if one of them were for me and if it was, who was going to drink the extra one? I heard him talking to another man, laughing actually. The sound was so alien to me; I could not recall a time when I heard him laugh. They walked in the kitchen, the other man and him. The other man was younger but had the same eyes. He was tall, thin, with lots of brown hair, kind of messy and wavy. When he saw me he smiled. He had a wide smile, showing bright white teeth and a dimple on one side of his face. His eyes were kind and he seemed genuinely happy to see me. How could a stranger be happy to see me when he didn't know me? "Hello, pretty girl! Aren't you the cutest thing? My name is Alex, what yours?" he said in a deep but friendly tone. By then I knew not to trust anyone in this house. I didn't respond and I didn't smile. My eyes followed his every move. Everyone sat at the table and began to eat breakfast cheerfully talking and laughing. What a strange phenomenon. I said I wasn't hungry and just sipped my juice, listening to their conversation and making sure not to smile when the stranger named Alex said something that was funny.

I learned that day that the stranger was their son. He was away at school and was only visiting for one day. He was leaving the next morning. He tried his best to talk to me and pay me attention. I was still skeptical but he seemed nice. He let me watch cartoons with him in the living room and we actually giggled at the same parts. By the afternoon I felt comfortable around him. We had ham and cheese sandwiches for lunch and he let me have some of his Coke. I wasn't allowed to have soda so that was a treat. Alex showed me how to play checkers and I even beat him once. Maybe he let me win but that was okay, I still won.

I was left alone for a while so I snuck into his room. I sat in the middle of the room on the floor. I did not want to touch anything so I would not get into trouble again. His room was tidy and dust free even though he was never home. Mrs. Carmen must clean it every day. It was a small room. There was only a full-size bed with a plaid blue comforter, a nightstand with a plain brown lamp with a beige hood. There was a dresser with colognes and deodorants, a brush and a small television set. There was no mirror, no knickknacks, and no posters on the wall, no pictures. That was very strange to me; it was like he really didn't live there at all.

Alex walked in and saw me sitting with my arms around my legs, my chin on my knees. With a curious look, he asked what I was doing. I didn't reply but suddenly hot tears began to fall. For some reason, his eyes began to water too and I felt that he understood my silent plea for help. He sat quietly next to me and pulled me towards him and I let him. I cried into his hug for a long time. He kissed the top of my head and told me that it would be okay. That whatever I was sad about would stop but that I had to be strong and do whatever I could to stop the bad. "How? How can I stop the bad?" I pleaded. "Be strong and just stop it. Ask for help if you need it. Tell your grandmother what is wrong. That's the only way to stop the bad. Tell her," he tried to convince me. I nodded with new resolve and with my shirt I wiped away at my tears. "Will you be here when I come back? I have five more days to be here. Please be here," I practically begged him. He shook his head no, gave me another kiss on top of my head and left the room.

Several times throughout the day, I would catch Mrs. Carmen's husband glaring at me. I wondered if I was doing something bad that would cause him to punish me. I know I was being respectful. I was being good. Wasn't that enough? I found him several times looking at his son while he talked or played with me. Why? I wondered. I also wondered why he couldn't be nice like his son. That evening I went home and I was actually happy. I really liked Alex. He was funny and kind and didn't treat me like I didn't exist. It was a good day. Too bad I would never see him again.

I woke the next morning to a warm and sunny day. It was Saturday and a perfect beach day. I asked if we could go but Mima was busy. Since she only had a week to go at the restaurant, she started selling and delivering clothes. That way she could make money and take me with her. She had a mountain of shirts, pants and dresses that she was sorting and getting ready for delivery. I was so excited when she told me I was going to help her collect the money! I helped her fold and package the items. She made a note of everything in a pretty notebook. Jotting down names, clothing items and the amount they cost.

All the things I found pretty I put to the side even though I did not know my size. I told her I was going to pay her with the money that I made working with her. She would make a pile of things my size. I got to choose what I wanted from what I called "my pile." Years later we still laughed about the money I owed her for the clothes I took. When it was time to make the deliveries, I helped pack the back seat of the car because of course I still rode in the hatchback. That was my spot. We worked till late into the night, delivering from house to house. I met a lot of ladies I had never seen before, some gave her the money there and others told her to come back on payday. Mima wrote everything in her notebook and we moved on to the next person. I was excited to be working with her and not having to go to a sitter.

Sunday came and knowing that the next day I would be going back there made me angry again. I still had five stupid days to go. I went outside and moped. I noticed holes in the dirt that reminded me of the crab caves, just smaller. Memories came like a tsunami and I shook with rage. I went inside the house and got the dish detergent. I squirted the detergent into every hole I saw and picked up a thick wooden stick. Placing the water hose in the holes, I filled it with water until the residents came out. Big, hairy, ugly spiders ran out of the foaming holes and I slammed them with the stick until there were no more spiders. I moved to the next hole and the next until I made sure all of them were dead. The entire time I wished it were he that I was squishing, he that was disappearing into bits. Once all the soap was gone and all the spiders were dead, I went into the house and got ready to face the week.

Monday morning brought no nice breakfast, no talking, and no laughter. I was told to sit in the corner of the living room and don't touch anything. Mrs. Carmen had to run errands and I was to stay behind. I begged to go with her but was told that I would slow her down. With a frown on my face, I sat looking out the window at nothing in particular. He sat on the sofa and turned on the television, and pretended like I wasn't in the same room, which was fine with me. I was counting the minutes until Mrs. Carmen came back. I kept glancing out the window but eyed him sideways to make sure he wasn't coming near me.

A few minutes after Mrs. Carmen left, I saw him rubbing the front of his pants so I turned away. When I heard him moan I looked again and he had his pants open, rubbing himself furiously. The faster he stroked, the louder he moaned. I tried to look away but was scared that he would try to touch me again. The next time I glanced his way, his eyes were open, non-blinking, bearing onto mine. He was making grunting sounds and breathing heavy. Beads of sweat were forming on his forehead, dripping slowly down the side of his face. Now I was terrified. What was he doing? What was he going to do to me? Maybe he was having a heart attack. I hoped he died. He stroked himself so hard and fast that I thought he was going to rip himself apart.

Then he spoke. "You like this, little girl? You see what you make me do? This is all your fault! You are a bad, bad girl," he said as his moans got louder. I couldn't look away; I was glued to my seat. My eyes wide with fear but I refused to cry. I kept telling myself I was strong and I was not a bad girl. I was a good girl and he was going to die. With a giant growl or maybe a howl, he stopped. I realized he made a mess of himself! He wet his pants. The wetness was on his shirt and all over his hand too. He got up to leave the room but turned and yelled, "You see what you made me do!" I didn't speak but in my mind I laughed. He wet himself, and it was not my fault. He wet himself and he did that all on his own. He was a dirty, nasty old man.

I was pretty sure that what he did was wrong but I was glad that he didn't touch me. I had to find a way for him never to touch me again. I didn't know how to stop him but I knew it was totally up to me. I had the power but I didn't know how to use it. I envisioned myself turning into Wonder Woman and tying him up with my lasso, punching and kicking him to the ground.

Wonder Woman was my hero. Mima had bought me the headband and cuffs and I used a rope as my lasso. I had my Wonder Woman Underoos, just twirling as hard as I could until I got dizzy, unleashing all my powers and running around the house, saving the world from monsters. My grand-mother would walk in on me and laugh. I would show her my fighting moves while she tried to keep a straight face. I was the defender of evil.

One evening, Mima asked me to take a plate of food to a neighbor, Ms. Maria. Ms. Maria was blind. She lived alone in a two-room dilapidated wooden hut with a tin roof. The hut had two cut-out square holes that were covered with plastic. Those were her windows. The door was a slab of wood held together by rusty hinges with no lock. The front room had an old table with two mismatched chairs. The counter was a slab of wood on top of cinderblocks. On the makeshift counter she had a few plates, bowls and silverware, and an old plastic cooler that looked as if it were kicked around in a game of soccer. Nothing matched and everything was old. The back room, where supposedly she slept, had a small mattress covered in an old blue quilt, one lonely flat pillow and a milk crate that served as her nightstand. This room had no windows or door. She had no electricity or running water and no propane for cooking. Her bathroom was called an outhouse. It was a small wooden structure with a chair that had a hole in the middle. I peeked in there once and was terrified. The hole was deep and dark and did not smell very good. I could imagine bugs and snakes coming out of that hole. I could imagine her falling into the hole and drowning in her own waste.

She was a robust lady with thick legs and arms, big hands smooth like a baby. Some said she was in her 80s, to me she was more than a thousand years old, ancient, maybe immortal. She was brown skinned, a face full of wrinkles with the biggest smile I had ever seen, long black hair with white stripes and matching white eyes. Her eyes followed you wherever you were even if you were quiet as a mouse; it was as though she could sense your spirit. One thing I knew for sure was that she could hear you. She turned to me as soon as I stepped onto her property.

Mima taught me to scream out her name so she wouldn't be scared and would know who came to see her. She received a lot of visitors. The entire town took care of Ms. Maria. They took her everything from food to medicine, frozen water in milk cartons and all her essentials. The townspeople would make sure she was safe when it stormed or when she was feeling ill, which was rare. In exchange, she let the kids pick fruit from her trees. Her land was large and full of mango, quenepa, and coconut trees surrounding her little hut.

Today I saw her look my way but instead of calling out to her I went straight to the quenepa tree and picked a few. I stood there eating them while staring at her silently. Her eyes still followed me. She knew someone was there but she remained still and quiet. Did she sense danger? I had yet not called out to her like I was supposed to.

I walked across her yard, eyeing her. Those white milky eyes following my every move. I waved and walked closer to the hut, taking my time and feeling mischievous. Maybe she could see and she was faking so people could feel sorry for her. Maybe she wanted people to take care of her. I stopped directly in front of the window and smiled. Quietly I crept in the kitchen and put down the food my grandmother asked me to deliver to her. I looked directly into her eyes, ran my fingers through her hair, touched her face and hands all while saying nothing. I knew I was being sneaky and disrespectful but I was curious about her in ways I had never been.

Ms. Maria's eyes still followed me as I touched her face. Quick as lightning she grabbed my hand and pulled me towards her. I jumped back and pulled her hair, hard. This caught her off guard and as she let my hand go to grab her head, I pulled her hair once more from afar and made her gasp in surprise. I turned and ran. I ran without stopping until I was home. Only then did I see a few long white strands entwined in my fingers. What I didn't realize was that I was laughing as I was running and that Ms. Maria heard me and knew exactly who I was. In hindsight, she probably knew it was I as soon as I stepped on her land. Also in hindsight, she never told my grandmother what I did that day. I don't know what was happening to me but I was becoming more daring, angry, meaner.

The next morning, I got into a rare argument with my grandmother. She was basically the only person I was truly happy with. It was unheard of me talking back or being ornery with her. This morning was different. I didn't want to get out of bed and didn't want to get dressed. I didn't like my clothes, the color was ugly, the material itchy, my shoes were lost, when found, they hurt my feet. Any darn excuse not to get dressed and out the house. I could tell my grandmother was getting wary of my attitude but I didn't care. She sat me down at the dining table and served me eggs and bacon like many days. Today the eggs were too soft and the bacon too salty. I spilled the orange juice and made no move to clean it up. For the first time that I could remember, she took the wet rag and flicked it at my leg. The sting was such a surprise that I wailed as if she had whipped me with a tree branch. I sniffed back tears the entire ride to Mrs. Carmen's. I was hurt and dejected. Mostly my feelings were hurt. Mima had hit me and that hurt my soul.

# Chapter Four

## ———— Beyond Mischief

Slamming the car door and stomping without a glance back was so unlike me. I surprised myself but again I no longer cared. This was a whole new feeling for me. I felt unloved, uncared for, confused but most of all hateful. The entire morning was uneventful, I refused to talk or eat. I sat on the floor in front of the sofa, not moving, staring out the window since they wouldn't even turn the television on for me. At least I was left alone, the way I wanted to be. The afternoon was another story. Mrs. Carmen fixed me a ham and cheese sandwich for lunch but I suddenly decided I did not like ham anymore. I took one bite and left the rest untouched. I asked for the forbidden soda and when it was denied I pitched a fit. Screaming that I wanted soda and not that nasty ham. My voice getting louder each time and each time I added unrelated text.

"I don't want that, I want soda!

Alex gave me soda, he was nice, and you are mean.

I said I want soda, the ham is nasty, and it tastes like your husband!

Give me soda; you are so ugly and fat.

You are fat and ugly and your husband smells!!"

This went on for a few minutes until I heard a door slam somewhere in the house. I instinctively knew that it was he.

Without a word he grabbed me by my arm and dragged me to Alex's bedroom. All the while I was kicking and screaming for him to let go of me, to leave me alone. Once in the room, he let go and I dropped to the floor as he closed the room door. I immediately knew something bad was going to happen and started screaming for Mrs. Carmen.

"Help me, Mrs. Carmen, he is going to hurt me.

He's going to hurt me again, please help me!"

My cries went unanswered.

He took off his belt, rolled me over on my stomach and swung it over my rear end. I screamed even louder but no one came, no one came to save me. He swung the belt again, bending down in the same moment. The next hit was with his hand stinging my butt. I embraced for more pain but his hits became softer instead of harder. His hits turned into fondling of my rear, his hands massaging me instead of inflicting pain. Was he trying to make me feel better? Was he trying to make the pain go away? My screams turned into loud sobs and hiccups.

"I don't want to hear you scream anymore or I will really beat you, do you understand?" he sneered. I hiccupped a yes as he stood and reached for the door. As he opened the door, I could see Mrs. Carmen standing right outside. Why didn't she come help me? She was there, hearing me scream for her and did nothing, at that moment I hated her as much as I hated him. They would pay for this. I would make sure I got even with them. I was going to hurt them as much as he hurt me.

I lay on the floor until it was almost time to leave. Mrs. Carmen had to come get me because I was not moving. She told my grandmother that I might be ill since I didn't eat my lunch. Ironically she didn't mention the beating, my screaming or that fact that I was in her son's bedroom all afternoon. Mima asked if I was feeling sick and I said maybe the ham made me sick. I no longer wanted to eat ham. "Silly girl, that's your favorite!" she mused teasingly. I think she was trying to cheer me up. Trying to determine the reason for my mood that morning and afternoon. "Well, I don't like Mrs. Carmen's ham and I don't want to eat there anymore. I will bring my own food." Pensively I also asked how many more days I had left and was delighted that there were only three more days.

To my surprise my grandfather was waiting for me when we arrived home. I ran out the car and jumped into his arms. He twirled me around so fast and high that I instantly became dizzy. Finally I was back to laughing uncontrollably. Once he put me down, I had to hold on for fear of falling while my head stopped spinning. This caused another fit of giggles. I called my grandfather Papi; that means "Dad" in Spanish. I did not remember much of my real dad and since my mother and aunt called him Papi, so did I. He didn't live with my grandmother but came to visit me every week. According to Mima, he was a ladies' man and that was why they were not together. I really didn't know what that meant at the time but I was used to married people not living together so I accepted it.

He was tall and handsome, always sporting a tan and always in his uniform. He was the Correctional Warden at the only prison in town. He had dark brown eyes, hair around his head but not on top and a trimmed mustache, no beard. He always smelled good, an earthy woodsy cologne that never changed. I cannot remember a time Papi was upset with me. His visits were full of candy, hugs, tickling and my favorite—coconuts and sugarcane.

The sugarcane he brought from the fields near his job. The prisoners would cut and sell the cane. Papi made sure to always bring me some. They looked like thick green tree branches. Papi would cut and peel them for me while I chewed and savored the sweet nectar. The coconuts were from our backyard. We had several coconut trees in the back but they were so tall that unless they fell on their own, we could not reach them. By the time a coconut fell off the tree they were old and dry. I loved the pure coconut milk inside. The coconut milk was not like regular cow milk, it was not white and creamy. It was clear and tasted like juice. Once the coconut milk was gone I would crack the coconut shell on the concrete and eat the inside, making sure I didn't eat it all or my belly would hurt. Papi would take off his uniform shirt, grab a huge machete and climb the coconut tree. I would laugh as he made monkey sounds. With one arm and his legs wrapped around the tree, he would pull himself up until he would find the perfect coconut. One good swing with the machete would make it fall. I watched and would run back and forth until the coconut would fall with a loud thump. Once he climbed down, he would take the machete and chop the top off. I would wait impatiently for the handoff so I could drink the milk.

"How's my Nena (little girl) doing?" he would ask.

"Papi, I'm fine but I don't like going to Mrs. Carmen's anymore. I hate it there but I only have three more days and I can stay with Mima for all the days."

"Why don't you like it there? I don't really like them but she was the only person that could take care of you. Do they treat you good? If not, tell me and I will take care of it." He was serious while telling me this, his lips a thin line.

I was really close to telling him what was happening but then I looked at his gun. He would take care of it, I knew. Probably shoot Mrs. Carmen and her husband right in the face. I found myself enjoying that thought but then wondered if Papi would get in trouble and instead of taking care of the prisoners; he would be inside with them. Then I would never see him again, and it would be my fault. I decided not to say anything.

"They are just old, Papi, plus they stink," I told him instead. He laughed then and I went back to eating my coconut, still thinking about the gun.

Spending the evening with Papi gave me the confidence not to worry about going to the sitter's. I felt ready to take on the day. Once again I was talkative during my ride, repeating jokes my grandfather told me the previous night, getting the punchlines wrong but still laughing at every joke. Mima laughing with me, pretending that she never heard the silly jokes, loving that I was acting like my usual self.

I lifted myself up and looked at my grandmother while she drove. "Mima, can Papi move back in?" I asked her. She peeked at me through the rearview mirror. Her only respond was "Hmmm." And I understood it was not up for discussion, so I lay back down.

The sun was shining, the sky was clear blue, the birds seemed to be flying along with the car and I felt wonderful. Little did I know that today I would have a hell of a fight on my hands.

Cheerfully singing to myself, I entered the kitchen, sat in my favorite chair facing the window and took out all my crayons and coloring books. "You are happy today, did something good happen?" Mrs. Carmen curiously asked. "Yes, my Papi came to see me and he is going to keep coming every day to make sure I am happy. We ate sugarcane and he showed me his gun," I said, adding extra punctuation to the word "gun." I wanted to make sure she heard that part. She wiped her hands on the apron while looking at me sideways and turned around, nothing else to be said. I continued to color and sing to my own tune, glad that the conversation was over.

Later that morning as I was still in my own little world of color and music, suddenly I felt the hair on the back of my neck stand, my chest tightened and I suddenly began to shiver. I heard him come out his room and I knew he was standing just outside the kitchen. I didn't have to look up to know he was looking at me. I could smell him. I could feel him looking at me. I began to choke and cough, losing my ability to breathe. The earlier bravado I felt left my body as tears stung my eyes. Mrs. Carmen began to pat my back and gave me some water to drink, causing me to choke harder.

"Let go of her, you don't know what you are doing. She needs to breathe," he snapped at Mrs. Carmen. In one swoop he picked me up over his shoulder and began to pat my back harder than she did. Meanwhile carting me to his room. As usual Mrs. Carmen did nothing.

"I have something that will make you stop choking. I know you were faking and you need to learn how to behave," he spat out once we were in the room. He threw me on the bed with one arm while slamming the door with the other. I felt my head spin when he turned the lock. I realized that Mrs. Carmen could not get into the room to help me, although instinctively I knew she would not either way. There was no use in screaming. I felt small and helpless but I refused to cry, to give him the satisfaction of my tears. I was not going to let him know I was terrified.

I knew he was going to hurt me again. This time I was going to show him that I was stronger than him. I was determined not to let him break me, it no longer mattered what he tried to do to me. I was going to fight. I tried to be brave and sneered at him, trying to scare him into leaving me alone until he began to unzip his pants. Then all my bravado left again and all I felt was a cold chill deep inside my small body.

I did not cry. I did not scream. I did not look.

"Open your mouth, open wide. And don't you bite me, leave your mouth open." His words were low and deep. I felt something on my lips and again he instructed me to open my mouth. I closed my eyes tighter and thought of a snake. A slimy, slithering, poisonous snake as it forced itself into my mouth. Slowly it twisted deeper and deeper until I felt it extending towards the back of my throat. I felt the snake's head move side to side, its tongue flickering inside my cheeks, trying to kiss my tongue, trying to become one. The snake began to go deeper. I was scared it was going to slide down into my stomach. I felt it trying to take over my body.

I began to gag violently, shaking and trembling with fear, disgust and finally rage. I felt a boiling fury within me. *No!* I screamed in my head. *This is not going to happen to me! I will not let him hurt me again.* I tried to shut my mouth as much as I could. The snake began to retreat as I closed my mouth tighter. I heard it whimper as it retreated so it must be hurt. Finally it recoiled and I managed to completely close my mouth as tight as my eyes. I could still hear it whimpering and imagined it slithering away, hiding from me.

It was a while before I opened my eyes slightly. I was still sitting on the edge of the bed, my mouth tightly shut. I wondered where the snake went. Was it under the bed? The bedroom door was ajar. Did the snake go to another part of the house? Would it try to bite someone else? Secretly I wished it was under the bed and it would bite the occupants during the night after they went to sleep. I slipped to the floor and looked around the room. Slowly I realized that there was no snake. It was all my imagination. That was my way of not accepting the truth. Now my tears came, hot and fast. Why was this happening to me?

I became aware that the whimpering had come from him, and what I thought was the snake slithering away was really his zipper being pulled up. He had left the room like a coward. I didn't know where he went or how long he was gone. But I knew that I had hurt him. I had hurt him and he ran away this time. This brought me pleasure. For once I felt my fear subside. For once I felt as though I had won.

I snuck out of the room carefully as I did not want to bump into him. As I made my way to the kitchen I noticed he was gone. Whether outside or truly gone, I didn't care as long as I did not see him again. Mrs. Carmen was sitting at the kitchen table. She eyed me sadly when she saw me take my seat quietly. It gave me satisfaction to see her looking sad. I enjoyed the idea of her crying. I wanted her to be miserable. I walked up to her and felt her face for wetness. Up close I could see the dry streaks down her face. I traced the streaks with my finger, one by one on both sides of her face. Her tears began to flow fast and warm on my fingers. Her shoulders began to shake uncontrollably. In between loud sobs she muttered, "I am sorry, baby, I am so, so sorry."

Incredulously I stared at her, she knew! She knew and did nothing. With the lightning speed of a cat, I scratched at her face. Leaving four thin bloody lines from her temple to her chin. She yelped and stood up so fast she knocked back her chair with a loud clatter. I smiled viciously at her while advancing toward her with closed fists. I wanted to pound her, hit her until she was bloody. I ran to her and pushed her as hard as I could. The wall saved her from falling but not from hitting her shoulder. She gasped in surprise, held her shoulder and her face simultaneously and ran out of the kitchen. I stood there and screamed. I screamed and screamed until I was hoarse. I screamed until I no longer had a voice. Then I went outside to wait for Mima to pick me up.

In my heart I felt stronger and braver. Somehow and unbeknownst to me, I was changing inside. I didn't know what it meant that day but later in life I would see it as a change from childhood innocence and mischief to a lifetime of hostility and defiance.

# Chapter Five
## ——————Making It Stop

Today was the last day! I was super excited and showed it. I was chatty the entire ride, asking what was the plan for the rest of the summer. It was now August and the weather was beautiful even though technically it was still hurricane season. Hurricane season in Puerto Rico is weird; one minute it's sunny with blue skies and the next it's gray with downpours. The hurricanes could be scary, especially since our house was a mile from the beach. I could stand on my roof and see the rain coming towards us like a curtain from the ocean, beautiful but oh, so dangerous. Today was the perfect mix of sun and breeze. As usual I was lying in the back of the hatchback thinking today was my last day in that hell of a place. I didn't have to see those people ever again.

Once I got to Mrs. Carmen's house, I kissed my grandma and I ran inside the house. Mrs. Carmen had ugly red scratches on her face that she tried to cover with makeup but it did no good. It gave me pleasure knowing that I did that to her face. I was glad she was hurt and looked ugly, hopefully they would not go away anytime soon. She didn't talk to me but I was fine with that. I decided to just look outside and daydream. I tried to think of happy things but the things that had happened to me in the last two weeks kept popping up in my mind. Every incident came at me like a huge sea wave knocking me over with every breath. How could he do that to me?

The more I thought about it, the angrier I became. So much happened in ten days. Ten days of pain. Ten days of keeping secrets. Ten days of me believing I had done something wrong to deserve what I got.

I had stayed up most of the night thinking about every single minute and realized that I didn't do anything wrong. I was not the bad girl he said I was. He was the bad one and he had to pay. I told myself I would never let it happen again. I would never let him hurt me again. I remembered how happy I was, always laughing and joking. Now I found myself distrustful of adults.

I was always friendly and talkative, now I had become suspicious of their intent. I no longer called the lunch lady for snacks, what if she tried to poison me? If I went to the restaurant where my grandmother worked, I would sit on the counter quietly eating my pie but no longer interested in what the waitresses were doing. I would stay close to my grandmother when we went to collect the clothes money. And I definitely did not talk to any man unless my grandmother said it was okay to do so. Now, most of the time I just stared or sometimes even glared at adults. And I blamed him for everything.

I never hurt anyone before so the thoughts that came to my mind both scared and exhilarated me. My daydreams were always about fun things that I wanted to do with my grandmother, things that I wanted to see and places I wanted to go, about love and fun stuff. Now I was thinking of ways I could hurt another person without getting caught and that jolted me out of my reverie. I had a sudden awareness that if someone hurt me, I had to hurt them back any way I could. I refused to be a victim. I don't think at that time I knew what a victim was but I did know enough where I wasn't going to let anyone hurt me again and that was a promise that I made to myself.

I looked up to see Mrs. Carmen staring at me. I became enraged. I jumped up and ran towards her with a speed unbeknownst to me. I pushed her as hard as I could. She yelped as her lower back hit the porcelain sink. I wasn't scared anymore. If anything, I wanted to be bad. I ran from the kitchen with no destination. I ran down the hallway and into the living room. I ran in circles screaming and then started swatting things to the floor. A maniac laugh erupted from me. The faster I ran, the louder I screamed and laughed. I knocked multiple knickknacks off the shelves and tables, hearing them shatter as I ran by. I ran back to the kitchen and knocked down my chair, hearing it clatter to the floor as I kept running. I don't know what came over me but it felt great.

Abruptly, someone yanked me off the ground by my hair. It happened so fast I swear my feet were still running. It could not be anyone else but him. He heard the racket I was making and came out of his room to see what the heck was all that noise. I began to kick and scream. Trying my best to hit him with my small fists. The more I struggled, the higher I felt my body go. The pain in my head was becoming unbearable and I felt myself sag.

"Let her go, you are going to kill her!" I heard Mrs. Carmen scream. I hit the floor like one of my old rag dolls. All I felt was a numbing pain as I tried to crawl to a safe corner. I saw him raise his fist and slam it into Mrs. Carmen's face. She screamed and fell to the floor next to me. He began to kick her in the stomach, her thighs and legs. She curled up in a fetus position to avoid the blows but that made him bend over so he could punch her again. After what seemed as an eternity, she stopped moving. I had managed to crawl to a corner of the living room, my back to the wall. Eyes wide as saucers, I watched him stand and stretch and then begin walking towards me.

For the second time in the same amount of days, he threw me over his shoulder and took me to the room, slamming the door closed with his foot. This time he threw me on the floor. I bounced up like a little mad animal and ran towards the door to try to get it open but he was faster than me. He slammed it again and this time he locked it and held it so I wouldn't get out. He was in my way, there was no way out. I ran towards him, punching and kicking just for him to push me down on the ground again. Then I remembered what hurt him the day before.

During my sleepless night it became clear to me that there were never any ants or snakes touching my body or in my mouth. My active imagination had played tricks on me. I was seeing and feeling things that were not true because I did not understand what was happening. There were no innocent caresses or protective embraces, no concern and definitely no interest in my wellbeing. I knew exactly what he did to me and I knew exactly how to hurt him now.

I stopped trying to fight him and sat on the bed. My chest heaving up and down from the exertion. I put my head down and let my hair fall over my face. He understood this to be a form of resignation but internally I knew what I had to do. I had to make him think I was giving up. I had to make him think he was going to win. Little did he know that I was a ball of rage about to explode, ready to take my life back. He remained against the door, catching his breath for a few minutes.

"Today is your last day and you think you can do anything you want? What the hell is wrong with you? Don't think that I am going to let you get away with what you did! I am glad that after today I will not have to deal with you," he said as he crept toward the bed. "Are you listening to me, little girl? Don't ignore me or I will punish you and punish you bad," he hissed.

I still had my head lowered but I was eyeing him through my hair. My brain was churning a plan and I needed him to be close, very close.

As he moved towards me, he was unbuttoning his pants, unzipping slowly. When he was a foot away from me, he pulled out his penis. Not ants, not a snake. I could see it through my hair. He pushed my head back and sneered at me. This time my eyes were open and I smiled wickedly back at him. I noticed him blink several times. Maybe he noticed my change; my steely resolve or maybe he could see the hate in my eyes. I was contemplating, waiting for my chance. There was no more fear or tears.

He held my head higher and tried to put his penis in my mouth. I would not open.

"Be a good girl and open up. Open up now," he demanded.

I cannot remember blinking as I stared at his face. I opened my mouth slowly. With a wolfish grin, he began to slide his penis in my mouth. I felt it touch my tongue and I almost gagged. I held the sensation and as he closed his eyes, I bit down as hard as I could! Time seemed to stop as his face registered what was happening. I saw the silent surprise and pain in his face. I bit down harder. A howl of a scream like an animal caught in a trap escaped his lips.

He grabbed my head with both hands and tried to remove himself from my grip. I bit harder as I had no intention of releasing him. It seemed to be a tug of war. The harder he tried to pull me off, the harder I bit down. He smacked me hard, his entire hand connecting with my face. The room began to spin as I fell sideways. I began to lose consciousness while still hearing his wails. Blackness came over me and then there was nothing.

I felt cool water on my face and began to wake. Mrs. Carmen was over me, wiping my face and my mouth with a cold rag. The rag was pink with blood. Her face was puffy and bruised. Her one eye swollen shut. "Wake up, Mija, you have to wake up so I can clean you up. You are okay. Wake up," she whispered.

My head was pounding and my face was on fire. I asked to go to the bathroom. She walked me and stood outside the door waiting. I peed and washed my hands. I happened to look up and saw my face. It was swollen on one side and flaming red. I checked for the blood that Mrs. Carmen was wiping from my mouth but I saw none.

I washed my mouth and spit out pink water. I kept spitting out water until there was no more blood. I ran my tongue around the inside of my mouth and over my teeth. There were no cuts, so where did the blood come from? Then I remembered. I remembered everything. I ran out of the bathroom and bumped into Mrs. Carmen. She never waited for me before so it was a shock that she was still there. I asked her where he was. She said he left and that he would not be back. She said I would never see him again and that I had nothing to worry about. Then she begged me to not tell anyone what had happened. She was crying uncontrollably and I knew that she was scared. She was scared of him. Mostly she was scared of me telling.

I am not sure if I felt bad for her or for myself but I made the decision not to tell. I told my grandmother that I was running, fell and hit my face. She was dubious when she saw Mrs. Carmen's injuries but she explained that she was in a fight with her now ex-husband. That she had called the police and had him arrested. She said she was pressing charges and that he would not be back. I wondered if he was taken to my grandfather's jail. Mrs. Carmen went on to say that I was a good child to take care of but that she was getting old and I would be the last child she would watch. She wished us luck and with a tight hug said goodbye.

I never saw her or her husband again.

# Chapter Six

#### —————— Summer

The rest of the summer was serene. I spent most of my days riding in the car with Mima as she fulfilled clothing orders and collected money. I helped her pack every order, after choosing what I wanted first. We became partners, closer than we ever were. Although I continued to be mischievous I never harmed anyone again. Overnight I returned to what I thought was my normal self. The funny, laughing and lovable little girl that everyone loved was back. However I was only truly lovable to my Mima and Papi, everyone else got a level of mistrust that was not there before.

I even went back to Ms. Maria's to take her food and frozen water in milk cartons. I would sit with her and listen to her stories. Sometimes I would make faces at her but I never touched her again. Honestly I never felt guilty or remorseful for what I did. If she knew it was me that awful day, she never told my grandmother. In my mind I would wonder what would happen if I moved some of her furniture. Would she trip and fall? Would she cry out for help and no one hear her? Would she know I did it? I thought about this every time I sat with her. I never acted on my thoughts but I admit I was curious.

As the summer came to an end, Mima started preparing for my departure. We would spend more time together. We would walk to the beach just to go to my favorite beach restaurant. It was more like a shack on the beach that sold fresh seafood caught by the local fishermen. We didn't love the beach in the traditional way. I feared the deep water and Mima hated the sun. So we would eat and walk back home to sit on the porch under the shade.

Then the dreaded call came from my mother with my flight information. I was to return back to Brooklyn, New York, in a few days. I would go from the salty fresh air of the beach to the pollution of the city. I would miss the quiet nights sitting on the porch drinking iced-tea. That peace would be replaced with noisy car traffic and screaming neighbors. The most I would miss was the long peaceful rides in the back of the hatchback while I daydreamed of a life that I would not have for many years.

# Epilogue
## ——— Going Home

I was surprisingly somewhat happy to be going home. I was going to miss my Mima dearly, especially since I knew she would be lonely without me. We usually both cried when she handed me over to the stewardess at the plane terminal. This time she cried alone. I told her not to worry, that I would be fine and that I would be back next summer. My heart, however, told me otherwise. I knew that I would never spend another summer with her in Puerto Rico. But it was okay, I was positive that we would see each other again. She would never abandon me.

I never spoke of what happened at Mrs. Carmen's house. I tried to pretend it never happened. I pushed it out of my mind whenever it tried to creep back in. I felt empowered that I stopped it. I stopped it by being strong and brave. No one would ever touch me again. I sat in the front row of the plane, eating my snacks and playing with my American Airlines wing pin. I didn't watch a movie this time. I just stared out the window at the blue ocean beneath the plane, looking for sharks, dolphins or maybe even a mermaid. The plane climbed higher and higher into the clouds. I wondered if I would see an angel sitting on one or jumping from cloud to cloud. Maybe they would wave at me or follow me home. No one would believe me if I told them I saw an angel, but it would be my secret. My secret to keep, like so many others.

# Omaira

Four hours later, the stewardess handed me over to my mother. She was tall and thin with short brown hair. She thanked the stewardess and took my hand to pick up my luggage. She did not ask how I was doing or how was my time in Puerto Rico. She didn't hug or kiss me like Mima did on a daily basis. She didn't even smile or look at me. And I wondered if she was even happy to see me. I realized then that I was a burden to her. Me spending the summers with my grandmother was her release. The vacation was more for her than me. I looked at her and realized how young she was. I now could see how I would be a hindrance to her. My mother was only fifteen years older than me. She was twenty and I was five. At that moment, I put my own mother on the list of adults that I didn't trust and unfortunately she would remain on that list for the rest of my life.

# Author's Notes

Where do I start? Probably from the part where I say I dislike talking about myself. That is probably the reason it took me so long to write my books. My memories have always been there. I mostly tried to forget or to pretend certain things did not happen. The memories come in bits and pieces, sometimes they come in harsh screams and other times as soft whispers but they are always there. Putting those memories on paper makes the demons real. Now that I am letting the demons lose, there is no stopping.

I was reluctant to share my stories. Yes, stories, plural. Although this is a work of fiction, it is still based on true events. I did not want to be defined by my past or the occurrences in my life. I now reflect back and realize that I had no control over some of these events. Others are debatable and many I am still coming to terms with.

It seems that my life was a tragic cycle of events. So many things happened that I never understood. There are so many questions that I still do not have answers for and I will most likely never get answered. My biggest question was always WHY? Through the years, I have learned that sometimes there are no answers to that why. Why me? Why not me? It's all the same.

It took me many years to love my life and accept that everything that I have been through made me the person I am today. My books are about innocence lost, sexual and mental abuse and the repercussions that those actions take in our lives.

Like I stated earlier, these stories are based on true events. The characters are real people. I have tried to remember as much as I can without hurting my psyche. I may have changed some events and names as some things still elude me. The earliest I remember about my life is at the age of five. I think that was the age where my life was defined or rather what I call the "beginning." I often wonder if the "beginning" had never happened, maybe the "end" would be different.

I was born in Puerto Rico and raised in Brooklyn, New York. I moved to Philadelphia, Pennsylvania, with my mother when I was just about to turn thirteen. I was reluctant to move to Philadelphia but I didn't have a choice. It was a tough transition but I made it. You will read about that transition in the next book.

It's been thirty-six years that I have lived in Philadelphia, and I can honestly say that the past sixteen have been the best years of my life. And life just gets better. That doesn't mean they were easy, far from it. I learned to love God and myself. Once I learned to love myself, I was able to love my family, as they deserved.

I live with my husband of thirteen years and our younger son. We have a combined family of three grown children and two grandchildren with one more that will be here by the time this is published. Oh, the excitement!

I love my life. I love my family. My grandchildren bring me so much joy and love. I can't see my life without them. However, my life wasn't always like this. I will take you through my journey and hope and pray that my stories can help someone.

Although initially reluctant to get my books published, I can't seem to stop writing now. One thing is certain: I would have never tried if Mima were still alive. If I decide to tell my full story, there will be several books. I do not know how this journey will end but hopefully we will see each other in my pages.

God Bless,
Omaira

Puerto Rico and New York sometime in the late 70s

Mima – You will forever be my heartbeat.

CPSIA information can be obtained
at www.ICGtesting.com
Printed in the USA
BVHW021146100122
625879BV00011B/172/J